THE BRAVE PIG *

LONG AGO, DURING THE REIGN OF BRAHMADATTA, THERE LIVED A CARPENTER IN A VILLAGE NEAR VARANASI.

EVERYDAY, HE WENT TO THE JUNGLE TO COLLECT WOOD. ONE DAY AS HE WAS RETURNING HOME...

OHH!

···HE TRIPPED OVER SOMETHING.

WHAT IS THIS? A PIGLET! POOR THING! IT MUST HAVE BEEN ABANDONED.

THE KIND-HEARTED MAN TOOK THE PIGLET HOME.

IT LOOKS SO FAMISHED!

YES, LET US GIVE HIM SOMETHING TO EAT.

TENDERLY THE COUPLE LOOKED AFTER THE PIGLET.

* BASED ON BADDHAKI-SUKARA JATAKA

1

HE SOON GREW UP TO BE A PLUMP FIERCE-LOOKING PIG WHO FOLLOWED HIS MASTER EVERYWHERE.

HA! HA! SEE HOW THAT PIG HELPS HIS MASTER. HE IS TURNING THE LOGS FOR HIM.

HE HAS LEARNT THE TRADE TOO. HE IS A CARPENTER PIG

LIKE A PET DOG HE LEARNT TO FETCH AND CARRY.

GET ME THE SAW, BADDHAKI.*

HE HAS GROWN QUITE BIG AND PLUMP AND SO HELPFUL. REMEMBER HOW TINY HE WAS WHEN I BROUGHT HIM HOME?

YOU HAVE TRAINED HIM SO WELL.

BUT WHAT IS THE USE? SOMEONE MAY BE TEMPTED TO KILL HIM FOR HIS MEAT.

* MEANS PIG IN PALI

THE CARPENTER HAD BECOME SO ATTACHED TO HIS PET THAT THIS THOUGHT HAD NEVER STRUCK HIM.

I CAN'T IMAGINE ANYONE KILLING HIM FOR FOOD.

YES! WE'VE BROUGHT HIM UP LIKE A CHILD. BUT TO OTHERS HE IS JUST A FATTENED PIG.

I FEEL HE IS NO LONGER SAFE HERE.

YES YOU ARE RIGHT. SOMEONE MAY TAKE HIM AWAY AND KILL HIM.

THEY DECIDED THAT IT WAS BEST TO RETURN THE PIG TO THE JUNGLE.

THERE! YOU WILL BE SAFER HERE. GOODBYE, BADDHAKI.

AT FIRST BADDHAKI FELT A LITTLE LOST IN THE JUNGLE HAVING LIVED SO LONG AS A PET. FOR DAYS, HE ROAMED ABOUT LOOKING FOR A PLACE TO LIVE. AT LAST HE CAME UPON A CAVE IN A HILLOCK.

THIS IS A GOOD PLACE. THERE IS A BROOK NEAR BY AND LOTS OF TUBERS TO EAT.

SOON HE FOUND HE WAS NOT ALONE IN HIS CHOICE OF A HOME. HUNDREDS OF PIGS ARRIVED THERE.

AH, THERE YOU ARE! I HAVE BEEN ALL OVER THE JUNGLE LOOKING FOR OTHER PIGS.

ARE YOU NEW TO THE FOREST?

YES, I USED TO LIVE IN THE VILLAGE WITH A CARPENTER. THAT IS WHY MY NAME IS BADDHAKI.

NOW I PLAN TO STAY HERE. IT IS AN EXCELLENT SPOT.

YES, BUT FRAUGHT WITH DANGER.

I WAS WONDERING WHY ALL OF YOU LOOK SO THIN AND WORN. AFTER ALL THERE SEEMS TO BE ENOUGH FOOD FOR ALL OF YOU AROUND HERE.

HOW CAN WE THRIVE? WE ARE FOREVER ANXIOUS AND WORRIED.

THERE IS A TIGER WHO ATTACKS US EVERY MORNING.

DOES HE COME EVERY DAY OR JUST OCCASIONALLY?

EVERY SINGLE DAY, AT SUNRISE.

HOW MANY TIGERS ARE THERE?

JUST ONE.

BUT THERE ARE SO MANY OF YOU. CAN'T YOU GET TOGETHER AND OVERPOWER HIM?

NO, NO. HOW CAN WE PIGS CONFRONT A TIGER?

ALL RIGHT. I SHALL HELP YOU TO CATCH HIM. BUT YOU MUST DO EXACTLY WHAT I TELL YOU TO DO.

WE WILL.

WE NEED A LEADER LIKE YOU.

THAT NIGHT BADDHAKI COLLECTED THE PIGS FOR A MEETING.

TO CONFRONT AND OVERPOWER OUR COMMON ENEMY, WE MUST PLAN OUR STRATEGY WELL.

HE IS NATURALLY STRONGER AND MORE FEROCIOUS THAN US. BUT OUR STRENGTH LIES IN OUR NUMBERS. WE WILL ARRANGE OURSELVES IN A PADMAVYUHA.

PADMAVYUHA?

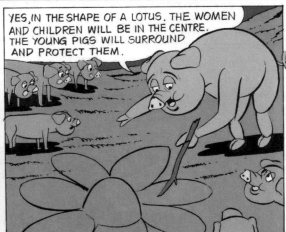

YES, IN THE SHAPE OF A LOTUS. THE WOMEN AND CHILDREN WILL BE IN THE CENTRE. THE YOUNG PIGS WILL SURROUND AND PROTECT THEM.

THE ADULTS WHO ARE FIT TO FIGHT WILL BE ON THE OUTER EDGE OF THE PADMAVYUHA.

I WILL STAND HERE. DIG A ROUND DITCH IN FRONT OF THIS SPOT. THE GROUND SHOULD SLOPE BEHIND ME. ON THE EDGE OF THE SLOPE MAKE ANOTHER DITCH MUCH DEEPER. IT SHOULD BE INCLINED AND FILLED WITH THORNY BRUSH AND SHARP STONES.

ALL NIGHT, THE PIGS WORKED HARD CARRYING OUT BADDHAKI'S INSTRUCTIONS.

FINISHED AT LAST!

IT IS ALMOST DAWN! TAKE YOUR POSITIONS.

AS USUAL AT DAWN THE TIGER ARRIVED TO CATCH HIS PREY.

OH! I AM FAMISHED. I MUST FIND A FAT PIG TODAY.

HE WAS SURPRISED TO SEE THE PIGS IN BATTLE FORMATION AND GLARED AT THEM IN ANGER.

HOW ODD! EVERYDAY THEY RUN AT THE SIGHT OF ME.

GLARE BACK AT HIM. DO NOT BE AFRAID.

THE TIGER OPENED HIS JAWS AND GROWLED LOUDLY.

GRRR...

THE PIGS GRUNTED TOGETHER IN REPLY.

GRRR...

OINK! OINK! OINK!

THE TIGER PRETENDED TO POUNCE ON THEM.

I WILL SCARE THE DAYLIGHTS OUT OF THEM.

ALL THE PIGS IMITATED HIM.

WHAT ON EARTH! THEY ARE NOT AFRAID OF ME AT ALL. THEY ARE IMITATING ME AS IF WE WERE PLAYING A GAME.

IT MUST BE THAT FAT PIG WHO IS LEADING THEM. I DARE NOT ATTACK THEM TODAY. THEY LOOK UNITED AND STRONG.

QUIETLY, THE TIGER SLUNK AWAY TO HIS CAVE. A WICKED HERMIT WHO LIVED NEAR BY SAW HIM.

WHAT? YOU HAVE RETURNED EMPTY-HANDED? WHERE'S YOUR PREY?

YES! YOU MUST BE LOOKING FORWARD TO YOUR USUAL SHARE OF PIG MEAT.

BUT BOTH OF US HAVE TO FAST TODAY.

WHY ARE YOU LOOKING SCARED?

THE TIGER SPOKE TO HIM ABOUT THE BEHAVIOUR OF THE PIGS.

DON'T TELL ME THE PIGS SCARED YOU OFF, HA! HA!

DON'T LAUGH AT ME. YOU SHOULD HAVE SEEN THEM TODAY.

ALL THESE DAYS THEY USED TO SCUTTLE OFF TO HIDE IN THEIR CAVES AS SOON AS THEY SAW ME.

AND TODAY?

9

BUT IN THE NICK OF TIME, BADDHAKI DUCKED AND JUMPED INTO THE DITCH AHEAD.

HAVING MISSED HIS TARGET, THE TIGER COULD NOT CONTROL HIS FALL. DOWN HE WENT ROLLING ALL ALONG THE SLOPE...

...AND FELL HEADLONG INTO THE DITCH DUG FOR TRAPPING HIM.

AHH!

THE TIGER WAS BADLY HURT AND INJURED BY THE FALL AND THE STONES IN THE DITCH.

BEFORE THE TIGER COULD RECOVER, BADDHAKI AND THE OTHER PIGS ATTACKED HIM...

BRAVO BADDHAKI.

... AND KILLED HIM.

WHEN THEY SAW THEIR ENEMY DEAD, THE PIGS SHOUTED FOR JOY.

YOU HELPED US TO KILL THE TIGER.

YOU ARE OUR TRUE LEADER, WISE AND COURAGEOUS.

THE DEER'S DISCIPLE ✳

THE KING OF KOSALA WAS VERY FOND OF HUNTING.

EVERY OTHER DAY HE WOULD GATHER HIS PEOPLE AND SET OUT ON A DEER HUNT.

COME, COME! THE KING WANTS YOU.

BUT I HAVE TO SOW MY FIELD.

MY COWS HAVE TO BE MILKED.

HOW DARE YOU DISOBEY THE KING'S COMMAND. COME ALONG.

OH DEAR, THESE DEER HUNTS ARE BECOMING TOO MUCH.

WE GO AWAY ALL DAY AND OUR WORK SUFFERS.

LET US THINK OF A WAY OUT.

THEY PUT THEIR HEADS TOGETHER TO FIND A SOLUTION.

IF ONLY THE FOREST WASN'T SO FAR OFF.

✳ BASED ON NANDIYA MIGA JATAKA.

I HAVE AN IDEA. LET'S MAKE A DEER PARK.

BUT WHERE?

IN THE SMALL WOOD NEARBY.

WE COULD DIG A LAKE THERE.

MAKE A FENCE AND A STRONG GATE.

THE TOWNFOLK WORKED HARD TO GET THE DEER PARK READY. TWO MONTHS LATER—

THERE! THE LAKE IS DUG AND FILLED WITH RAIN WATER.

AND THERE IS ENOUGH GRASS FOR SEVERAL DEER TO GRAZE.

NOW HOW WILL WE GET THE DEER HERE?

WE MUST GO TO THE DEEP JUNGLE WITH CLUBS AND DUMBBELLS.

ON THE APPOINTED DAY, THEY SET OUT TO GATHER THE DEER.

BEAT THE BUSHES TILL THE DEER COME OUT OF HIDING.

WE WILL HERD THEM BACK TO THE DEER PARK AND CLOSE THE GATE.

ARMED WITH WEAPONS AND ACCOMPANIED BY LOUD MUSIC, THE GROUP ENTERED THE JUNGLE.

A WISE YOUNG DEER NAMED NANDIYA SAW THE APPROACHING MOB.

THESE MEN APPEAR TO BE HUNTERS. I MUST TRY TO SAVE MY FATHER AND MOTHER FROM THEM, EVEN AT THE COST OF MY OWN LIFE.

HE RUSHED TO HIS PARENTS.

YOU TWO KEEP BEHIND THE SHRUBBERY. WHEN THE MEN COME IN THIS DIRECTION, I WILL SPRINT OUT. THE HUNTERS WILL COME AFTER ME.

AS HE HAD GUESSED, WHEN HE RAN OUT OF THE BUSHES, THE HUNTERS DID NOT SEARCH BEHIND HIM.

ANOTHER DEER CAME OUT FROM THIS BUSH. NOW LET US GO AHEAD.

GOOD! MY DEAR OLD PARENTS ARE SAVED.

ALONG WITH THE OTHER DEER WHO HAD BEEN ROUNDED UP, NANDIYA WAS LED TO THE NEW PARK.

COME, LET US TAKE THEM TO THE NEW PARK IN SAKET.*

OUR SON IS BEING TAKEN TO SAKET.

THE VILLAGERS RUSHED TO THE KING TO TELL HIM THE GOOD NEWS.

O KING! WE HAVE GATHERED SEVERAL DEER IN THE NEAR-BY PARK.

NOW YOU NEED NOT GO FOR HUNTING TO THE FOREST.

THE DEER GATHERED IN THE PARK REALISED THAT THEIR FATE WAS SEALED.

WE ARE ALL DESTINED TO BE KILLED SOONER OR LATER.

THE KING COMES AND SLAYS ONE OF US EVERY DAY.

AN OLD DEER SUGGESTED AN IDEA.

LET US ASSIGN TURNS. WE WILL FACE DEATH ONE BY ONE.

AGREED!

NANDIYA'S TURN WAS YET TO COME. HE SPENT HIS DAYS PEACEFULLY GRAZING IN THE PARK. BUT HIS PARENTS IN THE JUNGLE MISSED HIM. ONE DAY —

LOOK! THAT BRAHMIN APPEARS TO BE GOING TO SAKET.

IN A HUMAN VOICE THEY CALLED OUT TO THE TRAVELLER.

O BRAHMIN, IF YOU ARE GOING TO SAKET, TAKE A MESSAGE TO OUR SON IN THE DEER PARK.

CERTAINLY!

TELL HIM THAT HIS AGED PARENTS LONG TO SEE HIM.

I WILL DO SO.

THE BRAHMIN STOPPED AT THE DEER PARK.

WHICH ONE OF YOU IS NANDIYA?

ME!

THE BRAHMIN REPEATED THE MESSAGE.

YES, I COULD GO TO SEE THEM. I COULD EVEN JUMP OVER THE FENCE BUT I WILL NOT DO SO.

WHY NOT?

I AM INDEBTED TO THE KING FOR FEEDING ME FOR SO LONG. I ALSO HAVE A BOND WITH THE OTHER DEER HELD CAPTIVE HERE. I CANNOT RUN AWAY.

AS YOU WISH!

I WILL FACE THE KING'S ARROWS WHEN MY TURN COMES. THEN I SHALL DECIDE WHAT TO DO.

A FEW DAYS LATER—

IT IS YOUR TURN TODAY NANDIYA, TO OFFER YOURSELF AS THE KING'S VICTIM.

I AM READY.

THE KING NOTICED A REMARKABLE DIFFERENCE IN HIS VICTIM OF THE DAY.

EVERY DAY, THE DEER DESTINED TO DIE, RUNS HELTER SKELTER WHEN IT SEES ME AND SHIVERS IN ANTICIPATION OF HIS DEATH.

BUT THIS DEER STANDS CALMLY FACING ME, UNAFRAID OF HIS IMPENDING DEATH. HOW STRANGE!

THE KING STOOD WITH SURPRISE GAZING AT NANDIYA.

O KING! WHY DON'T YOU SHOOT YOUR ARROWS?

I CANNOT.

WHY NOT?

THIS ARROW, A LIFELESS PIECE OF WOOD, RECOGNIZES YOUR MERITS AND REFRAINS FROM HITTING YOU.

BUT I, A HUMAN WAS NOT ABLE TO APPRECIATE YOUR MERIT. FORGIVE ME.

GO, I WILL SPARE YOUR LIFE.

BUT WHAT ABOUT THE OTHER DEER IN THIS PARK?

I WILL SPARE THEM TOO.

WHAT OF THE OTHER BEASTS IN THE FOREST, THE FISHES IN THE SEA, THE BIRDS IN THE SKY?

I SPARE THEM ALL.

THUS GUIDED BY NANDIYA, THE KING MADE A PUBLIC PROCLAMATION—

LISTEN CAREFULLY, CITIZENS OF SAKET! HUNTING OF ALL ANIMALS IS HENCEFORTH BANNED IN THE KINGDOM.

FOR MANY DAYS, NANDIYA STAYED WITH THE KING, GIVING HIM WISE COUNSEL.

MODESTY, GENTLENESS, CHARITY, SACRIFICE, TENDERNESS FORGIVENESS AND NON-VIOLENCE — THESE ARE THE VIRTUES BEFITTING A KING.

ONLY THEN DID NANDIYA RETURN TO THE JUNGLE TO MEET HIS PARENTS.

THE GOLDEN CRAB *

TO THE EAST OF RAJAGRIHA THERE WAS A VILLAGE NAMED SALINDIYA. THERE LIVED IN THAT VILLAGE A BRAHMIN WHO DID FARMING. HE WAS A HAPPY, CONTENTED MAN AND SPENT HIS DAYS LOOKING AFTER HIS FIELDS.

ONE DAY—

IT'S SUCH A HOT DAY. I WILL REFRESH MYSELF AT THE POND.

AS HE SPLASHED HIMSELF, HIS EYE FELL ON A BEAUTIFUL GOLDEN BABY CRAB.

OH! HOW LOVELY!

HE LIFTED THE CRAB AND PLACED IT GENTLY IN HIS SHAWL.

LOOK WHAT I FOUND.

A GOLDEN CRAB!

HE WILL MAKE A GOOD COMPANION FOR ME.

HOW CAN A CRAB BE YOUR FRIEND?

ARE YOU GOING TO KEEP HIM IN YOUR HOUSE?

NO! HE WILL BE HAPPIER IN HIS OWN HOME IN THE POND.

* BASED ON THE SUVANNA KAKKATAKA JATAKA

BUT YOU MUST GET THEM FOR ME. I INSIST.

HOW CAN I ATTACK HIM? HE'LL DRIVE ME AWAY.

A SNAKE LIVES IN THE BAMBOO GROVE AHEAD. MAKE FRIENDS WITH HIM.

PERSUADE HIM TO BITE THAT MAN. THEN WHEN HE DIES FROM SNAKE BITE, YOU CAN GET HIS EYES OUT.

ALL RIGHT, I WILL TRY.

THE CROW BEGAN TO BEFRIEND THE SNAKE.

MY WIFE SENT THIS CHOICE MEAT FOR YOU.

OH, HOW DELICIOUS!

AS THE SEASONS PASSED—

THE CROP IS READY FOR HARVESTING, MASTER.

YES. HOW TIME HAS FLOWN!

YOUR PET CRAB HAS ALSO GROWN SO BIG MEANWHILE.

19

THE FRIENDSHIP BETWEEN THE CROW AND THE SNAKE HAD ALSO GROWN.

YOU DO SO MUCH FOR ME. I WOULD LIKE TO DO YOU A FAVOUR IN RETURN.

WILL YOU?

SURELY.

MY WIFE YEARNS FOR THE EYES OF THE MASTER OF THESE FIELDS. IF YOU BITE HIM, I COULD PLUCK OUT HIS EYES.

THAT IS EASY. I WILL DO IT TOMORROW MORNING. HE COMES EARLY BEFORE ANY OF HIS MEN.

I WILL HIDE HERE. THE BRAHMIN COMES THIS WAY AFTER REFRESHING HIMSELF IN THE POND.

AS USUAL EARLY NEXT MORNING THE BRAHMIN PICKED UP HIS PET CRAB FROM THE POND AND CAME TO THE FIELD.

JUST THEN —

AHH!

NOW I WILL GET HIS EYES AT LAST.

MEANWHILE THE CRAB CREPT OUT FROM THE SHAWL.

MY FRIEND IS IN DANGER.

AHH! MY FRIEND, THE SNAKE. WHERE ARE YOU? SAVE ME FROM THIS CRAB.

THE SNAKE TURNED BACK ON HEARING HIS FRIEND'S PLEA.

BUT THE CRAB WAS QUICKER AND GRABBED THE SNAKE TOO.

YOU DON'T EAT EITHER CROW MEAT OR SNAKE MEAT. THEN WHY DID YOU CATCH US?

TO PREVENT YOU FROM HARMING THIS MAN WHO IS MY FRIEND AND PROTECTOR.

EVERYDAY HE BRINGS ME FROM THE POND AND LOOKS AFTER ME.

SHOULD HE DIE OF SNAKE-BITE, MY LIFE TOO WILL BE IN DANGER.

SO MY ENEMIES WILL TRY TO KILL ME FOR MY TASTY AND TENDER FLESH.

THE SNAKE TRIED TO FOOL THE CRAB.

IF YOU ARE CONCERNED ABOUT THIS MAN, FREE ME. I'LL SUCK THE VENOM OUT FROM HIS BODY.

COME ON! HURRY UP AND FREE US. DON'T YOU KNOW HOW FAST THE VENOM SPREADS?

HE IS TRYING TO TRICK ME.

OKAY. I WILL LOOSEN MY HOLD ON YOU SO THAT YOU CAN MOVE A LITTLE.

BUT I SHALL NOT LET THE CROW GO TILL YOU CURE MY FRIEND.

THE CRAB HELD THE SNAKE BY HIS TAIL, ALLOWING HIM SOME FREEDOM OF MOVEMENT.

WHEN THE SNAKE SUCKED BACK ALL THE VENOM FROM THE BRAHMIN'S BODY —

AH! MY FRIEND HAS RECOVERED. THE POISON IS OUT.

BUT I CANNOT TRUST THESE TWO. THEY MAY ATTACK HIM AGAIN.

HE KILLED THE SNAKE AND THE CROW.

THE SHE-CROW TOO FLEW OFF.

THE PLACE IS NO LONGER SAFE.

BY THEN, THE HELPERS CAME TO THE FIELD.

WHAT HAPPENED, MASTER?

THE SNAKE BIT ME AND THE CROW WAS ABOUT TO TAKE OUT MY EYES.

BUT MY FRIEND THE CRAB, SAVED MY LIFE.

HE IS TRULY A FRIEND IN NEED.

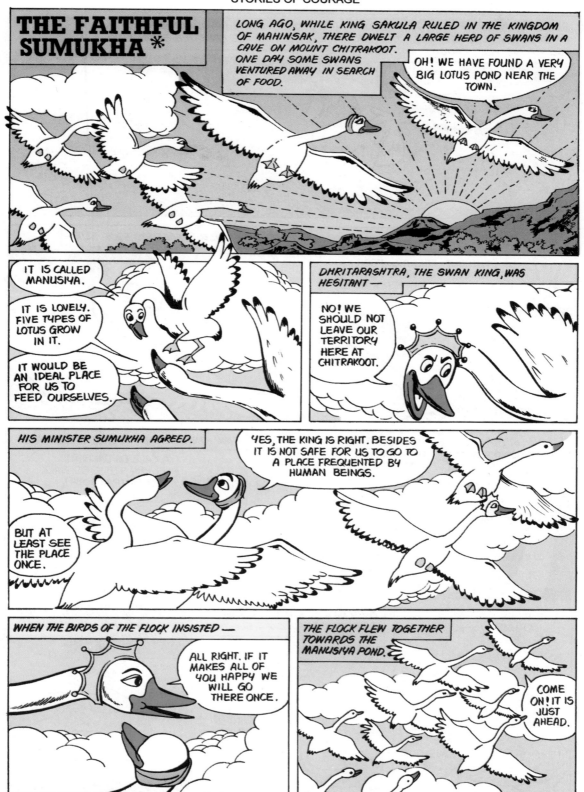

THE FAITHFUL SUMUKHA *

LONG AGO, WHILE KING SAKULA RULED IN THE KINGDOM OF MAHINSAK, THERE DWELT A LARGE HERD OF SWANS IN A CAVE ON MOUNT CHITRAKOOT. ONE DAY SOME SWANS VENTURED AWAY IN SEARCH OF FOOD.

OH! WE HAVE FOUND A VERY BIG LOTUS POND NEAR THE TOWN.

IT IS CALLED MANUSIYA.

IT IS LOVELY. FIVE TYPES OF LOTUS GROW IN IT.

IT WOULD BE AN IDEAL PLACE FOR US TO FEED OURSELVES.

DHRITARASHTRA, THE SWAN KING, WAS HESITANT —

NO! WE SHOULD NOT LEAVE OUR TERRITORY HERE AT CHITRAKOOT.

HIS MINISTER SUMUKHA AGREED.

YES, THE KING IS RIGHT. BESIDES IT IS NOT SAFE FOR US TO GO TO A PLACE FREQUENTED BY HUMAN BEINGS.

BUT AT LEAST SEE THE PLACE ONCE.

WHEN THE BIRDS OF THE FLOCK INSISTED —

ALL RIGHT. IF IT MAKES ALL OF YOU HAPPY WE WILL GO THERE ONCE.

THE FLOCK FLEW TOGETHER TOWARDS THE MANUSIYA POND.

COME ON! IT IS JUST AHEAD.

*BASED ON CHULLAHAMSA JATAKA.

SINCE MANY BIRDS USED TO FREQUENT THE LAKE, IT WAS A FAVOURITE SPOT OF BIRD HUNTERS TOO. WHEN THE FLOCK FLEW DOWN TO THE LAKE, THE SWAN KING FOUND HIS FEET CAUGHT IN A HUNTER'S NET.

AHH! I'M TRAPPED!

IF I CALL OUT NOW, MY COMPANIONS WILL FLY AWAY WITHOUT FEEDING. POOR THINGS! THEY HAVE FLOWN A LONG WAY TO REACH HERE.

QUIETLY HE TRIED TO FREE HIS FOOT BUT—

THE MORE I PULL, THE DEEPER THE NET CUTS INTO MY FLESH.

CALMLY HE WAITED.

AH! NOW THEY ARE PLAYING AND JUMPING ABOUT IN THE WATER. THEY MUST HAVE EATEN THEIR FILL.

THEN THEY HEARD HIS CALL OF ALARM —

AHH

A CALL OF DANGER! HURRY, LET'S GO BACK TO CHITRAKOOTA!

BUT WHO CALLED OUT?

NO TIME TO FIND OUT. WE MUST FLY OFF AND SAVE OUR LIVES.

ONLY ONE OF THE FLOCK WAS RELUCTANT TO FLY OFF—SUMUKHA THE MINISTER.

I CANNOT SEE OUR KING DHRITARASHTRA. IS HE THE ONE WHO IS WOUNDED?

WORRIED, HE RETURNED TO THE POND AND SAW THE WOUNDED AND BLEEDING KING.

DON'T WORRY, O KING, I WILL FREE YOU EVEN AT THE COST OF MY OWN LIFE.

BUT WHY DO YOU BOTHER? SEE ALL THE REST HAVE FLOWN OFF. WHAT HOPE IS THERE FOR AN ENSNARED BIRD LIKE ME?

I WOULD RATHER DIE WITH YOU THAN ABANDON YOU LIKE THIS.

BUT HOW WILL YOUR SACRIFICE HELP EITHER OF US OR ANYONE ELSE?

O FOREMOST AMONG BIRDS, IT IS MY DUTY TO BE WITH YOU NOW, IN THIS HOUR OF PERIL.

JUST THEN—

INDEED IT IS NOBLE OF YOU TO DO SO. I APPRECIATE YOUR DEVOTION TO ME. YET I GIVE YOU PERMISSION TO GO. SEE! THE HUNTER IS COMING THIS WAY.

WHAT LUCK! TWO SWANS ARE CAUGHT IN MY NET TODAY.

BUT WHEN HE WENT CLOSER—

YOU ARE FREE. WHY DON'T YOU FLY OFF LIKE THE OTHER SWANS?

I CANNOT DESERT HIM HE IS MY KING AS WELL AS A DEAR FRIEND. SET HIM FREE AND ALLOW US TO GO.

BUT YOU ARE FREE TO GO.

NO, I DON'T DESIRE FREEDOM FOR MYSELF ALONE. IN FACT I BESEECH YOU TO SPARE THE KINGS' LIFE AND CAPTURE ME IN HIS STEAD. I AM AS BIG AND FAT AS HE. IT WILL NOT MATTER TO YOU IF YOU CATCH ME INSTEAD OF HIM.

THUS WITH HIS GENTLE PERSUASIVE TALK SUMUKHA BROUGHT ABOUT A CHANGE OF HEART IN THE HUNTER.

I AM TOUCHED BY YOUR DEVOTION. GO I WILL SET YOUR KING ALSO FREE.

THANK YOU! MAY YOU ALSO BE HAPPY.

TENDERLY, THE HUNTER FREED THE ENSNARED SWAN'S FEET AND WASHED AND CLEANED HIS WOUND.

O KING, WE OWE THE HUNTER A FAVOUR FOR SPARING US. HE COULD HAVE SOLD US TO THE KING AS SHOW-BIRDS OR SOLD OUR FLESH. WHY DON'T YOU SPEAK TO THE KING ON HIS BEHALF?

TAKE US TO YOUR KING!

BUT THAT IS RISKY! THE KING MAY SELECT YOU AS A PET OR MAY HAVE YOU KILLED.

YOU HAD A CHANGE OF HEART. THE KING TOO MAY NOT BE HARD-HEARTED.

THE HUNTER TOOK THE BIRDS TO KING SAKULA.

HERE ARE TWO EXQUISITE SWANS, YOUR MAJESTY. HE IS THE KING OF SWANS AND THE OTHER IS HIS COMMANDER.

HOW DID YOU GET THEM?

WHEN THE HUNTER RELATED THE ENTIRE STORY —

LET THEM BE SEATED ON GOLDEN SEATS. BRING HONEY AND LUMP SUGAR FOR THEM.

AFTER THE SWANS WERE FED —

TELL ME WHAT CAN I DO FOR YOU?

O KING, THE HUNTER WAS KIND ENOUGH TO FREE US. WE CAME TO YOU TO GET A REWARD FOR HIM.

THE KING AGREED TO HIS REQUEST.

I GRANT YOU A HOUSE, A CHARIOT, GOLD AND AN ANNUAL INCOME OF ONE LAKH.

WITH THE PERMISSION OF THE KING SAKULA, THE SWAN KING DHRITARASHTRA AND SUMUKHA RETURNED TO THEIR HERD.

HOW DID YOU GET FREE?

IT WAS ENTIRELY BECAUSE OF THE WISDOM AND LOYALTY OF MY MINISTER SUMUKHA. HE RISKED HIS OWN LIFE TO SAVE ME.

Amar Chitra Katha's

EPICS & MYTHOLOGY

BRAVEHEARTS

VISIONARIES

FABLES & HUMOUR

INDIAN CLASSICS

CONTEMPORARY CLASSICS

EXCITING STORY CATEGORIES, ONE AMAZING DESTINATION.

From the episodes of Mahabharata to the wit of Birbal,
from the valour of Shivaji to the teachings of Tagore,
from the adventures of Pratapan to the tales of Ruskin Bond –
Amar Chitra Katha stories span across different genres to get you the best of literature.

21 Inspiring Stories of Courage

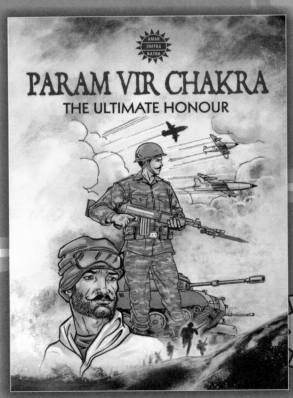